Encyclopedia Brown

and the Case of the
Secret UFOs

Encyclopedia
Brown
and the Case
of the
Secret UFOs

Donald J. Sobol

illustrated by James Bernardin

SCHOLASTIC INC.
New York Toronto London Auckland
Sydney Mexico City New Delhi Hong Kong

ISBN 978-0-545-41710-5

12 11 10 9 8 7 6 5 4 3   11 12 13 14 15 16/0

Printed in the U.S.A.   40

First Scholastic printing, September 2011

Designed by Jason Henry

For Jim Eiler and David Lile

CONTENTS

Encyclopedia Brown

and the Case of the
Secret UFOs

The Case of the Stolen Stamps

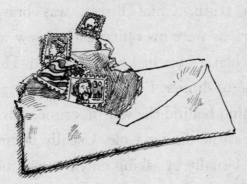

To a person passing through, Idaville looked like many seaside towns. It had lovely white beaches, four banks, three movie theaters, and two delicatessens. It was a wonderful place to live and work.

Unless you were a crook.

No one, grown-up or child, got away with breaking the law in Idaville. The reason for the town's spotless police record was to be found in a redbrick house on Rover Avenue. There lived Mr. and Mrs. Brown and their only child, ten-year-old Encyclopedia.

Mr. Brown was chief of police. He was always being praised for his work. It seemed no case was too tough for him.

In truth, Chief Brown was brave and smart, as were his officers. He knew what to do when a case had him stumped. He went home to dinner. Encyclopedia, the real mastermind behind the war on crime, solved the case at the dinner table. Usually before dessert. Usually by asking only one question.

The chief would have liked to give his son credit. He wanted to shout it from the rooftops or take out a full-page ad in the *Idaville News*. But even if he did that, what good would it do? Who would believe a ten-year-old boy could outsmart hardened criminals?

Besides, Encyclopedia wasn't looking for the extra attention. He was already a little different because only his parents and teachers called him by his real name, Leroy. Everyone else in town called him Encyclopedia.

An encyclopedia is a book or a set of books filled with facts from *A* to *Z*, like Encyclopedia's head. He had read more books than just about anyone, and he never forgot what he read.

One Tuesday evening at the dinner table, Encyclopedia was finishing his meat loaf. His mother was almost done eating as well, but his father's food was largely untouched.

Encyclopedia looked at his mother knowingly. If his father wasn't eating, it meant only one thing. A case was bothering him.

"I'm puzzled by this robbery that occurred yesterday," he said finally.

"What happened?" asked Mrs. Brown.

"Ten stamps were stolen from Terrence's Stamp Store," Chief Brown replied. "Mr. Terrence says they were collectively worth thousands of dollars."

"Was every stamp valuable?" Mrs. Brown asked.

Chief Brown checked his notes. "Mr. Terrence said the thief knew what he was doing. He didn't just grab what was handy.

"He took the most valuable stamps that

were on display. Three of them were from
Europe and over a hundred years old. Then
there were six American stamps, including
two that had printing mistakes in them. Not
many of those were made. Mr. Terrence says
that increases their value a lot."

"I wish my mistakes were valuable," said
Encyclopedia.

"Don't we all?" said Chief Brown.

"What about the tenth stamp?" asked Mrs.
Brown.

"That was just an ordinary stamp, the kind
we use every day." The chief smiled. "You'd
think Mr. Terrence wouldn't have even noticed that one being gone, but he's very careful with his records."

"Was there anything else taken?" asked
Mrs. Brown.

"Not that Mr. Terrence was aware of,"
Chief Brown said. "Some of the stationery
on his desk was disturbed, but he wasn't concerned about that."

"Do you have any suspects?" Encyclopedia asked.

"As a matter of fact we do," the chief replied. "We caught Red Finster near the store not long after the robbery was discovered. Red's known to fence stolen goods, especially small things that are easily moved. For him, stealing stamps is almost ideal."

"Except for what?" asked Encyclopedia.

"Except that he was clean when we nabbed him," Chief Brown explained. "We're holding Finster for questioning. Naturally, he says he's innocent."

"Did you search his home?" questioned Mrs. Brown.

"We did," said his father, "and that was a little funny. Usually, we need to get a warrant to do a search. But Finster said he had nothing to hide, and we were welcome to look. So we did."

"I guess you found nothing," Encyclopedia said.

"That's right. Even though we turned the place inside out."

"What if he had a partner?" asked Mrs. Brown. "Somebody who helped with the robbery and now is holding the stamps until the case cools."

Chief Brown shook his head. "Finster has a long record, and he always works alone. He doesn't trust anybody. We're going to have to let him go tomorrow if we don't find some proof linking him to the crime. I can't think of anything that will turn up that fast. We might catch him later, of course, when he tries to sell the stamps. Who knows how long he'll wait? Or where he'll try to sell them. Stamps aren't like stolen cars. They're pretty easy to keep hidden."

Encyclopedia closed his eyes. He always did his deepest thinking with his eyes closed.

Suddenly, he opened them. "Was any of the stationery missing?"

"I don't think Mr. Terrence paid any

Encyclopedia closed his eyes. He always did his deepest
thinking with his eyes closed.

attention," Chief Brown said. "There were papers and envelopes scattered all around. He was focused on the stamps."

Encyclopedia nodded. "At least you can hold Red Finster till the end of tomorrow," he said.

"By law we'll have to release him after that," Chief Brown said.

"Don't worry," said Encyclopedia. "You're not licked yet. By then you'll have the stamp of approval you need."

WHAT MADE ENCYCLOPEDIA SO SURE?

(Turn to page 75 for the solution to "The Case of the Stolen Stamps.")

The Case of the Secret UFOs

In the summer, Encyclopedia ran his own detective agency out of the family's garage. The Brown Detective Agency was well known throughout the town. Every morning, Encyclopedia Brown hung out his sign right after breakfast:

BROWN DETECTIVE AGENCY
13 Rover Avenue
Leroy Brown, President
No case too small
25¢ per day
plus expenses

It usually didn't take long for a new client to appear.

This time it was Flash Borden who came running up. Flash was in fifth grade, like Encyclopedia. His real name was Gordon. He had left Gordon Borden behind in kindergarten. Flash, he had decided, suited him better.

He wasn't called Flash because he could run fast. The name had stuck to him because he was a big fan of flash photography. He liked to take pictures at night. Flash had the best collection of bat and owl photographs in Idaville. He was known for his patience and for not being afraid of the dark.

Flash stopped to catch his breath. "I d-don't have much time," he gasped.

"Why not?" asked Encyclopedia. "Is someone chasing you?"

"No, no, not that."

"Then what's wrong?" Encyclopedia asked. Flash took a deep breath. "I just don't want to be late. Bugs Meany is selling pictures of unidentified flying objects, and I want to buy one."

Encyclopedia frowned. Bugs Meany was the leader of the gang of older boys, the Tigers. They should have been called the Shepherds. They were always trying to pull the wool over someone's eyes.

Encyclopedia spent a whole lot of his time stopping their attempts to take advantage of the kids of the neighborhood.

"Are you sure the pictures are real?" said Encyclopedia.

"No, I'm not," Flash admitted. "Frankly, I'd give anything to be able to take a picture of a UFO myself. I don't even know how to look for a UFO. Having one of those pictures will be the next best thing."

He plunked a quarter down on the empty gasoline can that Encyclopedia used as a counter. "I have to be careful not to buy a fake. Bugs's pictures are pretty expensive.

That's why I want you to come with me."

"Fair enough," said Encyclopedia. "Let's go see if those pictures will fly."

They found Bugs Meany outside the Tiger clubhouse, an empty toolshed behind Mr. Sweeny's Auto Body Shop. He had set up his pictures on a small table.

There were several shots of a flat round object sailing high in the air. The shots had been taken from different angles, though they all showed the same spaceship—if that's what it was.

"Step right up," said Bugs. "Buy yourself a genuine photograph of an unidentified flying object. Are aliens spying on us from outer space? Should we be worried or welcoming? You be the judge."

Several kids were looking at the pictures.

"The spaceship is kind of blurry," said one kid.

"Of course it is," said Bugs. "Those aliens were not just standing around saying 'Cheese!' They were probably on a secret mission, traveling at hypersonic speed."

"Hypersonic?" said another kid. "I've heard of supersonic, but what's hypersonic?"

"It's something we don't have," Bugs explained. "I mean, the aliens have to be able to get here from some other planet, right? They can't do that using the kind of speed we have here on earth."

He paused for effect. "They need something faster. That's what hypersonic is. Considering how fast their ships go, we're lucky to have any images of them at all."

"I guess that makes sense," said the first kid. "But how do we know these spaceships are real? They don't seem to have any weapons or antennas sticking out."

"Of course not," said Bugs. "That would not be aerodynamic. All those things are pulled in when they're not in use. The aliens don't want a bumpy ride while traveling millions of miles through space. I don't blame you for being suspicious."

Bugs cleared his throat. "That's why we

only got pictures that are clearly stamped USAF in the lower left corner. That stands for the United States Air Force. Now, it's one thing to accuse me of faking a picture. Man, oh, man, it would be unpatriotic to accuse the United States Air Force of doing that."

Two of the Tigers stood up straight and saluted into space.

"No, no," said the first kid. "I am patriotic! I was just asking to make sure."

Bugs nodded. "Of course you were. Okay, who wants to collect a piece of history? Ten dollars apiece, that's all I'm asking."

The kids moved forward for a closer look.

The Tiger leader was wound up, talking a mile a minute.

"Note that the picture even has the date and time it was taken: June twenty-fourth at 4:47 P.M.," he declared. "You can't get more precise than that."

Flash held up one of the pictures. The spaceship itself was a little blurry, but the date and time were perfectly clear.

"That proves it, right?" Flash whispered to Encyclopedia. "The pictures are just what Bugs says they are."

Encyclopedia took a look for himself. "If any aliens were checking us out," he said, "they weren't doing it from this spacecraft. This picture is a fake."

Bugs looked shocked. "Are you accusing the United States Air Force of something underhanded?"

"Actually," said Encyclopedia, "I'm doing just the opposite."

WHAT DID ENCYCLOPEDIA
MEAN?

(Turn to page 76 for the solution to "The Case of the Secret UFOs.")

The Case of the
Scrambled Eggs

Bugs hated Encyclopedia. His plans to cheat the children of the neighborhood were always blocked by the boy detective.

Bugs dreamed of getting even. A good poke on the nose was worth trying. That is, until he thought of Sally Kimball.

Sally was Encyclopedia's junior partner in the Brown Detective Agency. She was also the best athlete in the fifth grade.

Bugs didn't care about any of that.

What he did care about was Sally's punching power. He felt it for the first time when she had defended a boy Bugs was bullying.

She jabbed with a left to the nose, followed by a right to the belly.

Bugs made a crash landing in the grass. "Send in the cavalry," he groaned.

Afterward he insisted she had caught him cold. He didn't have time to warm up.

"You have to watch out for Bugs," Sally often reminded Encyclopedia.

"He's not happy about you, either," Encyclopedia said.

A few minutes later, who should show up at the garage but Bugs himself. He was carefully carrying a carton of eggs. Sally immediately jumped to her feet.

"Now, now," said Bugs, "there's no need to get excited. I came here to get some help."

"You did?" said Sally.

"Really?" said Encyclopedia.

Bugs nodded. He took out a quarter and slapped it down on the gasoline can. "There! You see? It's official."

"Tell me more," said Encyclopedia.

"I want you to guard these eggs for me this

morning," Bugs said. "At one o'clock, meet me at the corner of Main and Elm Streets."

"That's it?" said Encyclopedia.

"Yup," Bugs said. "If you think you can handle it."

"Why hire Encyclopedia?" asked Sally. "Why not use one of your Tigers? You're all in the same gang. Don't you trust them?"

"Of course I trust them," said Bugs. "But they're all busy doing their homework or helping little old ladies across the street. I thought anybody with a problem was welcome here."

"May I see the eggs?" asked Encyclopedia.

"Be my guest," said Bugs. He opened the carton, which was filled with eggs. "Take a look."

Encyclopedia took a look. The eggs seemed perfectly ordinary. He picked one up. It felt perfectly ordinary, too.

"I know what you're thinking," said Bugs. "What's so special about these eggs? I'll tell you. It's personal, very personal. You don't need to know anything else to do the job. Will you help me or not?"

"Sure, Bugs," said Encyclopedia. "You can depend on me."

Bugs smiled broadly. "Great. I'll see you later. Remember, one o'clock. Don't be late."

And off he went.

"I'll bet there's something rotten about these eggs," said Sally.

Encyclopedia shrugged. "Maybe Bugs is trying to turn over a new leaf."

Sally was not convinced. "If Bugs turned over a new leaf, I'm sure it would be blank."

Encyclopedia kept an eye on the time. At 12:45, he left the garage. Sally remained behind in case any new clients came by.

It was hard for Encyclopedia to believe there were any egg thieves hot on his trail. Still he stayed alert just in case. As far as he could tell, though, no one paid any attention to him.

At one o'clock sharp, Encyclopedia showed up at the corner of Main and Elm, as he had promised.

Bugs was coming toward him, crossing the street with a policeman.

"There he is, officer!" cried Bugs.

"Yes, I see," said the policeman.

"Just like I told you," Bugs went on. "See that carton of eggs? I was suspicious when I saw him carrying it. He didn't have a whole bag of groceries or anything. Only the eggs. I followed him to see what he was up to. What did I see? He threw two of the eggs at the windows of a house."

"I did?" said Encyclopedia.

"Uh-huh," said Bugs.

"Why would I do that?" questioned Encyclopedia.

Bugs laughed. "Why would you do it? That's easy. You're trying to create business for yourself. Somebody wants to know why eggs are being thrown at their windows. So they come to you to figure it out. Bingo!

"There he is, officer!"

You've got yourself a new case. Of course, you can't point the finger at yourself. You'll have to frame some innocent bystander."

Bugs rolled his eyes at the policeman. "This just gets worse and worse."

"You do make it sound pretty bad," said Encyclopedia.

Bugs took a bag out of his pocket. "I've even got pieces of the two eggshells as evidence."

"This is a pretty serious charge," said the policeman.

"Caught in the act by an eyewitness!" Bugs howled triumphantly. "Do you have anything to say in your defense?"

"I have eggsactly one thing to say," said Encyclopedia. "I'm innocent."

HOW DID ENCYCLOPEDIA PROVE IT?

(Turn to page 77 for the solution to "The Case of the Scrambled Eggs.")

The Case of the
Roman Pots

"Is this the Brown Detective Agency?" a girl asked, entering the Browns' garage.

"It is," said Encyclopedia. "And you're Julie Benson. I saw your picture in the newspaper last year. You found those arrowheads up by Indian Point. As I recall, you were able to date them as being over two hundred years old."

Julie smiled. "You remember quite a bit. I heard you had a good memory." She took out a quarter and placed it on the gasoline can. "I need your help. I'm still very interested in archaeology. I want to collect old things, not just arrowheads, but things from all over the world."

"That's a great hobby for a fourth grader," Sally remarked.

"I'm always on the lookout for a chance to add to my collection," Julie said. "There's a boy at the high school, Gus Anthony, who put up signs saying that he will be selling ancient Roman pots. I don't think I'll be getting to Rome any time soon, so I'd love to buy one. The thing is, I don't know much about ancient Rome. I figure you know."

"I've read a little," said Encyclopedia. "When is the sale?"

"This morning," said Julie.

"Then let's go," Sally said. "With luck, we'll be able to figure out if Gus is a crackpot or not."

Gus Anthony had set up shop in his backyard. Over one shoulder he wore a sheet, which was tied with a rope around his middle.

Encyclopedia, Julie, and Sally joined the other kids who had come for the sale.

Sally giggled. "Why is he wearing that outfit?" she whispered.

"It's supposed to be a toga," Encyclopedia explained. "It was a comfortable form of Roman clothing. I think Gus is trying to build the proper mood. He's wearing a laurel wreath on his head, another Roman tradition. It was kind of their version of a hat."

Gus bowed to the crowd of children. "Thank you all for coming to this special sale. Julius Caesar, the great Roman general, was famous for saying: *Veni, Vidi, Vici.* That's Latin. Translated into English, it means: *I came, I saw, I conquered.* Today, I hope that some of you will end up saying: *I came, I saw, I bought some pots.*"

He pointed to the table in front of him. Several pots of different sizes were on display. They were blackish-brown in color and irregular in shape. They certainly looked made by hand.

"See how the glazing is worn?" said Julie. "And the edges are chipped. You'd expect that on pots people used two thousand years ago."

"These pots," Gus said, "served a number of purposes. The tall one might have held wine. The short, fat one with the lid could have held honey. The small ones would have been used for spices. The Roman Empire spread over thousands of miles, and the people of Rome were able to buy things from all over the known world."

The kids looked impressed.

"Of course," said Gus, "it's not enough that the pots are old. Just being old, after all, covers a lot of ground. The pots are more valuable when they're dated. Now you have to remember that the ancient Romans did not use the same numbers that we do. We use the Arabic number system. They used their own system, which we call Roman numerals." He lifted one pot to show everyone the bottom. "You can see this one is dated XXIII B.C. XXIII means twenty-three."

"That's over two thousand years ago," said a boy in the front row.

"Right you are, kid," said Gus. "Which is very old by anyone's standards. That's the reason the pots are expensive. They'd cost a lot more if you had to buy them in a store. They're pretty delicate. Look, but don't touch."

"What do you think?" Julie asked Encyclopedia. "He certainly sounds like he knows what he's talking about."

"It might have helped if he had known a little less," said Encyclopedia. "Rome wasn't built in a day, and none of these pots were around when it was."

HOW DID ENCYCLOPEDIA KNOW?

(Turn to page 78 for the solution to "The Case of the Roman Pots.")

The Case of Grandma's Cookies

Ziggy Ketcham was the most absentminded boy in Idaville. Everyone knew that. Even Ziggy had known that before he had forgotten it.

Right now he was trying to remember what had brought him to Encyclopedia Brown's house in such a hurry. He knew he had been in a hurry because he was out of breath from running. He just didn't remember why he was in such a hurry.

"Can I help you, Ziggy?" asked Encyclopedia. He had been watching his friend standing outside his garage for a while. Encyclopedia knew Ziggy well enough to know that when Ziggy stood around like that, it meant he had forgotten something he was trying to remember. Encyclopedia also knew that Ziggy liked to remember things for himself. However, sometimes he needed a little help.

"I know I came here for a reason," said Ziggy. "It's not an accident. I wanted to hire you, I think. That's why I'm holding this quarter."

He came forward and put it on the gasoline can.

"That's a start," said Encyclopedia. "There's no extra charge for helping you remember why you wanted me to help you in the first place. It's all part of the service."

Ziggy looked relieved. "Thanks, Encyclopedia. Where do we start?"

Encyclopedia thought for a moment. "Don't worry about remembering everything at once. We'll chip away one memory at a time."

"Chip!" Ziggy shouted. "That's it. I remember now. You're brilliant, Encyclopedia. I came here to get you to help me get back some stolen cookies. Chocolate chip cookies. My favorite kind. My grandmother sent them to me from California. Nobody makes better chocolate chip cookies."

"How did you lose them?" asked Encyclopedia.

Ziggy closed his eyes. "The cookies came in the mail today. They were sealed in a metal tin. I ate a couple right away—they were as good as ever—and then I closed up the tin to save the rest for later."

"And?" asked Encyclopedia.

"And what?" said Ziggy.

Encyclopedia smiled. "I think you were starting to tell me how your cookies were stolen. But we haven't gotten to the stolen part. What happened next?"

"Oh, right. Let me see . . ." Ziggy scratched his head. "I was sitting on my front steps. The tin was on the step beside me. Then Rocky Graham came by on his bike."

Encyclopedia nodded. Rocky Graham was a member of the gang of tough boys, the Tigers.

"What happened next?" Encyclopedia asked.

"Rocky saw me with the tin," Ziggy said. "He asked me what was inside it. I told him cookies. Then he asked me if he could have a glass of water. I went inside and got it. When I came back out, he drank the water and went on his way." Ziggy frowned. "It was only after he was gone that I realized the tin was gone, too."

"Are you sure you didn't bring it into the house when you went to get Rocky his drink?"

"I thought of that," Ziggy answered. "I've looked everywhere to be sure. The tin is gone. I haven't been anywhere else, except to come here."

"Well, well," Rocky sneered, "if it isn't Mr. I-forget
and Mr. Know-it-all."

"Did you talk to anyone else about the cookies?" Encyclopedia asked.

Ziggy shook his head. "He was the only one."

Encyclopedia nodded. "Then I think we should go pay Rocky a visit."

They found Rocky lying on his front lawn, chewing on a blade of grass.

"Well, well," Rocky sneered, "if it isn't Mr. I-forget and Mr. Know-it-all. To what do I owe the pleasure of your company?"

"We're investigating a crime," said Encyclopedia.

"You took my cookies!" Ziggy blurted out. "I want them back."

"Me?" Rocky looked shocked. "I know I may have done a few things in the past. That doesn't mean I'm guilty of anything now."

"Oh, yes, it does," Ziggy insisted.

Rocky laughed. "Listen, Amnesia Boy, you wouldn't remember your own name if your mother hadn't sewn it in your underwear. So how could you remember anything I might have done?"

Ziggy reddened. "Why, you—"

Encyclopedia put his hand on Ziggy's shoulder to calm him down. "You'll have to forgive my friend," Encyclopedia told Rocky. "As you can see, he's pretty upset. Who wouldn't be? The missing cookies are his favorites. His grandmother sent them."

"Sure," said Rocky. "I've got a grandmother, too."

"Of course you do," said Encyclopedia. "Now, I'm not accusing you of anything. Since Ziggy mentioned that you had passed by his house, I was hoping you might have seen something."

"You mean like a witness?" Rocky asked.

"Exactly," said Encyclopedia. "Some kind of clue that will point us in the right direction."

Rocky grinned. "No problem. I want to help. Now that you mention it, I did see a kid hanging around. Nobody I recognized though. He might have taken your tin. He looked kind of suspicious. I think he headed off toward the beach."

"Can you give us a description?" Encyclopedia asked.

"Well, I wasn't paying close attention. Tall and skinny, maybe, with brown hair."

"Wow," said Ziggy. "That's really nice of you to help like that. I'm sorry I yelled at you before."

"Forget it," said Rocky. "I just hope you can find the kid before it's too late—and all your chocolate chip cookies are gone. "

Encyclopedia turned to Ziggy. "You see," he said. "I knew Rocky would help us." He turned back to Rocky. "Now I know you took the cookies. I just hope you didn't eat them all yet."

WHAT WAS ROCKY'S MISTAKE?

(Turn to page 79 for the solution to "The Case of Grandma's Cookies.")

The Case of the Grabbed Groceries

Idaville looked very festive as Encyclopedia walked through the center of town. It was the Fourth of July weekend, and American flags lined the edge of the town park, fluttering in the breeze. Above the storefronts, red, white, and blue bunting was hanging from every window.

The town celebration was always a lively one.

"Oh, Encyclopedia!" said a voice from the other side of the street. "Thank goodness you're here."

Ginger Bailey, a seventh grader, was the one calling out. She worked hard as a volunteer. Nobody helped out more than Ginger.

She glanced both ways and then crossed the street to Encyclopedia.

"What's the matter?" he asked. "You look upset."

"That's because I am upset," said Ginger. "Somebody just stole the groceries I bought for the barbecue on my block. I need to hire you to get them back."

"Where did this happen?" Encyclopedia asked.

"In the grocery store. I had just paid for everything, and, was heading out, when I remembered I had forgotten the mustard. So I put my bag down on the counter near the exit. Then I went back for the mustard. I wasn't gone more than a minute. When I got back, my groceries were gone."

"What had you bought?" Encyclopedia asked.

Ginger looked at a list she was carrying. "Hamburgers and hot dogs, rolls and buns to go with them, bags of potato chips, and cans of soda."

"Nothing special there," said Encyclopedia. "Were there any witnesses?"

"I asked the clerk, but she had been busy helping another customer. The store manager was in his office the whole time."

"What about other customers?" asked Encyclopedia.

"The only person I saw in the store was Rusty Malone."

"Rusty Malone?" Encyclopedia frowned. Rusty was a member of the Tigers. They were all so crooked they couldn't walk in a straight line.

"After you noticed the bag was missing, did you ask Rusty if he had seen anyone take it?"

"No, I couldn't," Ginger said. "He was gone, too."

"How long ago did this happen?" Encyclopedia asked.

"Maybe ten minutes."

"Come on, we don't have a moment to lose," said Encyclopedia. "If we don't act fast, your evidence will be gone forever."

When they arrived at the toolshed that was the Tigers' clubhouse, a few of the Tigers were putting charcoal on a grill. Rusty himself was out front, doing push-ups.

". . . ninety-eight . . . ninety-nine . . . one hundred." After this last one, Rusty got to his feet.

Ginger pointed to a table next to the grill. "There are my groceries."

"You mean our groceries," Rusty snapped. "Me and the boys are going to have a barbecue."

"With my food!" cried Ginger.

"Excuse me," said Rusty. "I didn't realize you were the only person who ever thought of having a barbecue over the Fourth of July weekend."

"That's not what I meant," said Ginger. "I had just bought those groceries. You were there in the market. You saw me."

"Maybe I did," said Rusty. "That's not a crime. I went in to see if we needed anything else for our barbecue. Turns out we didn't."

"If you weren't buying groceries when I saw you," Ginger went on, "where did these come from?"

"Ooooh!" said Rusty, "you got me. Unless, of course, I bought the groceries earlier today. That's what I did, right, boys?"

"Right, Rusty," the Tigers said together.

"See," said Rusty, grinning. "No mystery here."

"You have exactly the same things that I bought," said Ginger. "How do you explain that?"

"I can't," said Rusty. "It's a . . . what do you call it, fellows?"

"A coincidence."

Rusty nodded. "Exactly."

Encyclopedia wasn't done yet. "You look out of breath, Rusty," he said. "The way you would look after running over here with a bag of groceries."

"Hey, I'm just a little winded from doing all those push-ups. It's important to stay in shape, you know," Rusty crowed. "I've got other exercises to do. Now take off before I make you the crunch of the week."

"Not quite yet," said Encyclopedia. "You must be thirsty after working out so hard. You should have a drink. Luckily, you have all those cans of soda."

Rusty looked at the cans. "Don't want one," he insisted.

"Oh, come on," said Encyclopedia. "Here, let me help you." He pulled one of the cans loose.

Rusty backed away a little. "I said I didn't want one. Now put it back."

"What can we do?" asked Ginger. "It's his word against mine."

"I think we can do better than that," said Encyclopedia. "Rusty is more shook up than you think."

HOW DID RUSTY GIVE
HIMSELF AWAY?

(Turn to page 80 for the solution to "The Case of the

Grabbed Groceries.")

The Case of the Giant Shark Tooth

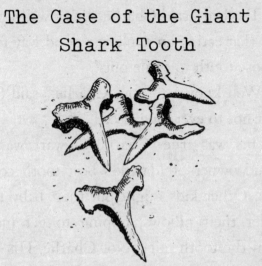

Encyclopedia Brown was eating an apple when Charlie Stewart walked into his garage.

"Ah," said Charlie, "you must have a loose tooth."

"Don't jump to conclusions," said Encyclopedia. "Appearances can fool you. Every detective knows that."

Charlie looked disappointed. "You mean you don't have a loose tooth?"

"Afraid not," said Encyclopedia. "The truth is, I just like apples."

"Too bad," said Charlie. "It's a well-known fact that eating an apple is a good way to get a loose tooth to come out."

"Well known to you, Charlie," said Sally, "but not to everyone else."

This was true. Charlie Stewart was the proud owner of Idaville's best tooth collection. Other kids might put their baby teeth under their pillows, hoping to get money from the tooth fairy. Not Charlie. His baby teeth were the first things he had collected. He kept them in a display at home, each one labeled with the date it had fallen out. Although he also had a bear tooth, a lion's tooth, and a rattlesnake fang, he wasn't satisfied. He was always on the lookout for new teeth to collect.

"Haven't found any hen's teeth yet, have you?" Sally asked.

Charlie laughed. "That would really be something. As I suspect you already know, hens don't have teeth."

"Beaks don't count?" said Sally.

"Not the same at all," Charlie insisted. "Sharks do have teeth. Rows and rows of them. That's why I'm here. Duke Kelly, one of Bugs Meany's Tigers, is selling what he says are the largest shark teeth ever. If it's true, I just have to have one. It would be the star of my collection."

"Duke Kelly's family has a boat," said Encyclopedia. "I don't know how many fish stories they have to go with it."

"Neither do I," said Charlie. He put a quarter down on the gasoline can. "That's why I want to hire you to come with me. Duke says he's selling the teeth for a good cause. The children's hospital in Cincinnati will get the money."

Sally snorted. "The only place the money will go is into Duke's pocket."

"That may be," said Charlie, "but a chance to get a special shark's tooth is too good to pass up."

"We'll soon find out," said Encyclopedia, "one way or the other."

Duke was making his pitch down at the dock by the marina. A crowd of young boys and girls listened to what he had to say.

"Glad to see so many of you believe in me," he began, "because this is a once-in-a-lifetime opportunity. That doesn't come around very often." He glanced at Encyclopedia and Sally. "I'm sure there are a few doubters here, too. They're welcome. Who knows, maybe they'll see the error of their ways."

Sally folded her arms.

"So let me explain," Duke went on. "My uncle is a deep-sea fisherman. It's cold, back-breaking work, but he loves it. It's a life of adventure and surprises."

"I wonder if he isn't really a pirate," Sally whispered.

"Sometimes, the surprises aren't good

ones," Duke went on. "Last week my uncle had one of the worst surprises ever. He was about six miles out when he hooked an enormous shark on one of his lines. The shark didn't give up. It pulled and thrashed for hours. Three times my uncle thought the fishing line would break. Three times the line held. Finally the shark wore itself out. Or at least that's what my uncle thought. He reeled it in. As he was lifting it onto the deck, the shark started thrashing again. My uncle jumped back to safety. Some parts of his boat were not so lucky. The shark crushed a few things on the deck before he finally stopped moving. It was nine feet long from nose to tail, with the fiercest teeth my uncle had ever seen. Luckily, he recognized that this shark was really old. Because it was so old, it had really large teeth. He sent me a box of them to sell."

Duke reached down into a box at his side and pulled out a long white tooth.

"Whoa!" said Charlie. "Look at the size of that thing."

"Scary, eh?" said Duke. "Even from a distance, you can see how jagged it is. You shouldn't wonder at that. Given everything a shark chews on, you'd expect a lot of wear and tear."

"That doesn't count the things it swallows whole," Charlie whispered.

Duke walked around with the tooth, making sure everyone got a look. "Sharks' teeth like this are pretty rare. That's why I'm asking ten dollars apiece. That's a real bargain for something this unusual."

A lot of the kids came forward to stand in line.

Even Sally was a little impressed.

Charlie, though, could barely contain himself. "Wow! This is really amazing. A tooth like that would be the highlight of my collection. Right, Encyclopedia?"

"A shark tooth is certainly worth having," Encyclopedia answered, "but in this case, I wouldn't bite."

WHY NOT?

(Turn to page 81 for the solution to "The Case of the Giant Shark Tooth.")

The Case of the
Missing Medallions

Chief Brown picked up Encyclopedia one night at the library. "Did you get all the information you need for your report about dinosaurs?" he asked.

"I think so," said Encyclopedia.

His father smiled. "Have you solved the mystery of why they disappeared?"

"Most experts think a comet was responsible," Encyclopedia said. "It hit the earth about sixty-five million years ago. The explosion filled the air with superheated clouds that changed the climate and the landscape, so that the dinosaurs could not survive."

"Do you believe that?"

"I do," Encyclopedia said, "and I feel sorry for the dinosaurs. They never knew what hit them."

Suddenly, the police radio started crackling.

The chief picked up the receiver. "This is Chief Brown," he said. "Go ahead."

The dispatcher told him there was a robbery in progress at a shop in town called the Den of Antiquities.

"I'm on my way," said the chief.

Encyclopedia had heard his mother mention the shop. It had only been open a couple of months. The owner was a man named Roger Cuthbert. His ads in the *Idaville News* claimed that his shop featured rare and valuable artifacts from around the world.

The Den of Antiquities was on a side street near the harbor. It had a fancy dark green sign with gold lettering above the entrance.

Roger Cuthbert was standing out front. He was holding Winslow Brant roughly by the arm.

What's Winslow doing here? Encyclopedia wondered.

Winslow Brant was Idaville's master snooper. The city dump was his home away from home, and he had never met a trash barrel he didn't like. Moreover his snooping had a purpose. He could see value in other people's junk. He could find an antique needle in a haystack if he knew he could sell it at a profit.

Chief Brown and Encyclopedia got out of the squad car.

"Thank goodness you're here, Chief," said Mr. Cuthbert. "I caught this young scoundrel in the act."

"Mr. Cuthbert, let's back things up a little," said Chief Brown, "and I think you can let go of Winslow. He's not going anywhere. Are you, Winslow?"

"No, sir."

"Why don't we continue this conversation inside?" said Chief Brown. "Watch your step everyone. Stay clear of the broken glass."

Inside the shop, Encyclopedia took a careful look around. The shelves were lined with small clocks, carved wooden boxes, porcelain figurines, brass lamps, and other collectibles. On the floor were a spinning wheel, spindle-backed chairs, some rolled-up oriental rugs, and a few small tables.

"Tell me what happened," said the chief, taking out his notebook.

"I had closed up for the day," Mr. Cuthbert said, "and was updating my accounts. I still had some work to do, but I decided to get a cup of coffee at the restaurant around the corner. I was only gone a few minutes. When I got back, this boy was standing in front of my shop, and one of my windows was broken." He pointed to the broken glass on the sidewalk. "See that display case inside the

*"When I got back, this boy was standing in front of
my shop, and one of my windows was broken."*

window? I had three ancient Roman medals, called medallions, there. Now they're gone."

"I didn't take them," said Winslow. "I'm innocent."

"Oh, really?" said Mr. Cuthbert. "Were you innocent earlier this afternoon when you came into my shop?"

"I was just curious," said Winslow. "The shop has a lot of nice things."

"Especially the medallions," said Mr. Cuthbert. "Do you deny asking to hold them?"

"No," said Winslow.

"Where are they now?" asked Mr. Cuthbert.

"I don't know," said Winslow. "All I did was come by for another look. When I got here, the window was broken and the medallions were gone."

"Will you empty your pockets, Winslow?" Chief Brown said.

Winslow did as he was asked. He took out three bottle caps, a rusty skate key, and a bottle opener.

"Is that all?" asked the chief.

"Not quite," said Winslow. From his other pocket he took out a fountain pen and a bent spoon. "I did some collecting on the way here," he explained.

"No medallions, though," said Encyclopedia.

"That proves nothing," said Mr. Cuthbert. "Maybe he stashed them somewhere before I grabbed him. Or maybe he had a partner in crime."

"Is anything else missing?" the chief asked.

Mr. Cuthbert glanced around the shop. "I can't be sure without a thorough examination. It doesn't look like the rest of the shop was disturbed." He pointed a finger at Winslow. "He knew exactly what he wanted."

"How valuable were the medallions?" the chief asked.

"Taken together? Perhaps a few thousand dollars," Mr. Cuthbert replied.

Winslow whistled. "I've never found any-thing like that at the dump."

"No, I imagine you wouldn't," Mr. Cuth-bert said. "That's why you robbed me. I caught you red-handed, boy. You watched me leave for the restaurant. You came up to the window. Maybe you hesitated at the last sec-ond, I don't know. Whatever, the lure of the medallions was too strong for you. You broke the window, reached in, and stole them."

"Winslow's always made his money fair and square," said Encyclopedia.

"Only because he's never been tempted before," said Mr. Cuthbert.

"Don't you worry," said Chief Brown. "I'll get to the bottom of this."

"As far as I'm concerned, the case is closed," Mr. Cuthbert said. "Now, if you don't mind, I have some plywood in the back that I can use to board up that window until I can get it fixed. If you could just wait here while I get it, I'd feel much safer."

"Of course," said Chief Brown. He closed his notebook as Mr. Cuthbert disappeared. "It doesn't look good, Winslow."

"I never stole anything," Winslow said glumly.

Encyclopedia had closed his eyes to think. Now he opened them. "Actually," he said, "I have a pretty clear idea who the thief is now."

"You mean you've cracked the case?" said his father.

"You could say exactly that," said Encyclopedia.

WHO WAS GUILTY OF THE THEFT?

(Turn to page 82 for the solution to "The Case of the Missing Medallions.")

The Case of the Shipwreck

Sally fanned herself because of the heat in the Brown Detective Agency.

"We ought to open a branch office at the beach," she said. "I'm sure the beach has mysteries all the time."

"It's a thought," Encyclopedia said.

"We could be missing out on something big," Sally insisted.

Encyclopedia went so far as to say only, "The heat must be the record for this day of the month."

"If the temperature goes up another degree, I'm going to melt," Sally said, and took a swig of bottled water.

Penny Nichols, a fourth grader, came up the driveway. "Thank goodness you're here!" she declared. "I was afraid you might be at the beach trying to beat the heat."

"We would be if we had any sense," Sally said.

"What can we do for you?" Encyclopedia asked.

Penny laid a quarter on the gasoline can. She didn't let go of it, though, not for a second. Penny didn't part with her money easily.

"We're hired," said Sally. "Tell us the problem."

"Wilford Wiggins has a once-in-a-lifetime opportunity for anyone with a little extra cash," Penny informed them

"Wilford?" Encyclopedia groaned. "Oh, not Wilford again!"

Wilford Wiggins was a high school dropout and as peppy as a pillow. He couldn't stand to watch people work before noon.

"I'm saving myself until something important comes up," he explained.

His chief exercise was trying to swindle the little neighborhood kids out of their savings. Happily, Encyclopedia was there to halt his phony big deals. Only last week the detective had stopped him from collecting money to manufacture a new-car smell. It was for people who want to smell like a new car.

"Wilford is holding a secret meeting today at five o'clock at the city dump. It's just for little kids," Penny said.

"It's nearly five now," Sally said. "We better get going if we want to hear his latest big deal."

When they got to the dump, a crowd of about twenty little kids was waiting, eager to learn how they could get rich quick.

Wilford stood on a rusted washing machine. "Gather round. Hurry, hurry, hurry. Time is money. I'm glad all my little friends could make it. Your faith in me will be rewarded—if you tell no one. I don't want grown-ups reaching the treasure first."

The children made anxious noises, fearful for the money they didn't yet have.

"Your treasure is safe if you don't speak of it," Wilford said. "Loose talk is dangerous." He motioned the children to come closer. "I have an uncle who lives down at the southern tip of South America. Last week it was really hot there, kind of like today. He went to the beach to cool off."

"Smart man," Sally muttered.

"He was standing at the edge of the water," Wilford continued, "when a sea chest washed up onto the shore. The chest held tools and several gold coins. My uncle is convinced there's a shipwreck nearby. It could be a pirate ship or one of those treasure galleons that sailed the waters hundreds of years ago. Considering the coins he found, he figures there's a fortune on board. It's waiting at the bottom of the sea."

A scattering of "Ooohs" and "Ahhhs" rose from the children.

"I got excited, too, when I first heard my uncle talk about a wreck," Wilford confessed. "He said a lot of ships went down in those parts during the 1600s and 1700s. Spanish ships and ships of other countries sailed there loaded with gold bars, coins, and jewels worth millions, and sank."

"I have a question," Penny asked. "Wouldn't it be easier for your uncle to borrow money from grown-ups he knows?"

"An excellent question," Wilford said. "I asked him the same thing. He explained that if he tells anybody about the sea chest, they'll start looking for the ship themselves. So he has to keep it a secret. That's when he thought of me. He figures that his secret is safe this far away. At the moment, he doesn't have the money to hunt the ship. He hopes he can still get the money he needs from me and my loyal little friends."

"Why don't you loan him the money your-self?" asked a boy.

"My money is tied up in oil wells," said Wilford. "So I'll tell you what I'm going to do. I'm going to make you rich beyond your wildest dreams. Buy a share in the sunken treasure ship for a measly five dollars. It will return you ten times or even a hundred times that amount when my uncle finds the ship."

Ten times! A *hundred* times!

The crowd of children buzzed with excitement.

"What do you think, Encyclopedia?" Sally asked.

The boy detective shook his head. "I think Wilford's shipwreck won't hold water," he said.

WHAT WAS THE CLUE?

(Turn to page 83 for the solution to "The Case of the Shipwreck.")

The Case of Mrs. Washington's Diary

The Idaville flea market was open every Saturday in the summer. It was held in the vacant field behind the library. The vendors sold everything from secondhand furniture to old sets of china and silver.

Encyclopedia and Sally were moving slowly down one of the aisles, checking out things in the different booths. They passed leather-bound books and old maps of different states.

"There has to be something here," said Sally. "I'll know it when I see it."

"Don't worry," said Encyclopedia. He turned over a cut-glass bowl.

"That's easy for you to say," said Sally. "You're not the one whose mother is having a birthday tomorrow. You're not the one who still doesn't have the perfect present."

"True," said Encyclopedia. "I'm also not the one who waited till the last minute to shop for her."

"I know, I know," said Sally. "Don't remind me. I'm sure I'll find something. My mother loves American history. Around here, there's plenty of history, though most of it is a bit dusty and crumpled. That only proves that it's old."

They passed a booth featuring cast-iron pots and pans hanging on a string. They were jet black and encrusted with a layer of hardened grease.

"These look very old," said Encyclopedia.

"I don't think that kind of history would

appeal to her so much," said Sally. "Let's keep looking."

The booths were laid out in rows, and the detectives carefully went up and down each one. A couple of times they stopped to look at something closely, but there was always a problem of one kind or another.

They had come about three quarters of the way through the market. Sally was beginning to get a little nervous when they saw a high school boy with a booth of his own. A few younger kids were looking at some old toys on his table. There were three yo-yos, some tops, and a wooden chess set that somebody's dog had chewed.

"Step right up," said the boy. "My name's Jack. Jack Higginbottom. I've got a lot of treasures here from my attic. My family has lived in Idaville a long time, so there's plenty to see."

"I didn't know kids could rent space here," said Sally.

"Oh, sure," said Jack. "Everybody's welcome."

Sally picked up a brass letter opener. "Do you have anything really old?" she asked. "Anything historical?"

"I do," said Jack. He opened an old box. It was filled with papers. They were all yellowed and brown around the edges. "I hadn't taken these out before," he explained, "because I didn't want the wind blowing them around."

"Those do look old," Sally said.

"More than two hundred years old," said Jack. "You're looking at pages from the diary of George Washington's mother."

The other kids at the table all stopped what they were doing to listen.

"Her name was Mary Ball Washington," Jack continued, "and she was quite a lady. Born in 1708, she was the second wife of George's father, Augustine. They got married in 1730."

"That's all true," said Encyclopedia.

"Of course it is," said Jack. "Mary, as I like to call her, had a strong opinion of herself. Women in those days, however, weren't allowed to speak their minds, and so she kept a diary. Now, if I had the whole thing, it would be worth a lot of money, but I only have a few pages."

"That sounds perfect," said Sally.

"I have to admit," said Jack, "that most of the pages are concerned with everyday things like chores and life on the farm. By far the best page is the one she wrote the day after George was born."

"What does it say?" asked Sally.

"I'll read it out loud," said Jack. "If you don't mind, I'll handle it myself. The page is pretty delicate." He carefully looked through the papers in the box. "Ah, here it is. Now, it's not a long entry—which is understandable considering that Mary was still recovering from giving birth. These are her words:

I am so impressed looking at little George lying in his cradle. Augustine and I have a feeling he is destined for great things. Why, I wouldn't be surprised if someday he grew up to be president. I only hope I live long enough to see it.

"That's amazing," said Sally.

"Believe or not," Jack added, "she actually did live that long. Mary Ball Washington died in 1789, a few months after her son George was inaugurated the first president of the United States."

"That's true," said Encyclopedia. "I'm sure she was very proud."

Sally could barely contain her excitement. "That's the one I want! I just hope I can afford it."

Jack smiled. "I'm sure we can work out something. I want that page to find a good home."

"My mother will be so excited," said Sally.

"That's the one I want! I just hope I can afford it."

"Right, Encyclopedia? Isn't it just perfect?"

Encyclopedia took a long look at Jack. "I cannot tell a lie," he said finally. "The diary is a fake."

WHY WASN'T ENCYCLOPEDIA FOOLED?

(Turn to page 84 for the solution to "The Case of Mrs. Washington's Diary.")

Solution to *The Case of the Stolen Stamps*

Encyclopedia wondered why an ordinary stamp would be stolen along with the rare ones. He also wondered why a knowledgeable thief would waste his time disturbing some stationery. Then he realized that the thief had taken something else, something Mr. Terrence hadn't noticed—an envelope.

The thief took the envelope and the ordinary stamp so that he could mail the rare stamps home to himself as soon as he left the store. That way if he was caught, he would have nothing on him. When Chief Brown checked Red Finster's mail the next day, he found the stolen stamps delivered in an envelope just as Encyclopedia had predicted.

Solution to *The Case of the Secret UFOs*

There was nothing about the alien spacecraft itself that showed the picture was a fake. The problem surfaced when Bugs said the pictures were taken by the air force. The air force, as a branch of the military, uses military time, which doesn't start the time again at noon, as standard time does. In military time 2:05 in the afternoon would be 1405. If the picture had truly been photographed by the air force, the time cited would simply have read 1647. Since the pictures were stamped 4:47 P.M., Encyclopedia knew that Bugs made the pictures himself. When Encyclopedia explained this, Bugs confessed.

Solution to *The Case of the Scrambled Eggs*

Bugs claimed that he had been following Encyclopedia around ever since he saw him carrying a carton of eggs. If Encyclopedia had egged the two house windows, he should only have ten eggs or fewer left in the carton. But Encyclopedia knows he still has the full twelve. Bugs said that he was watching Encyclopedia the whole time, and so Encyclopedia couldn't possibly have added any more eggs to the carton. When Encyclopedia explained this and showed the policeman the full carton, Bugs confessed to attempting to frame the detective.

He had to clean both the windows at the house as punishment.

Solution to *The Case of the Roman Pots*

Gus did a good job of sharing many facts about ancient pots and Roman times. However, he went a little too far when he started talking about dates. While it's true that the Romans used Roman numerals, Encyclopedia knew that they never put B.C. on anything. B.C. was only created hundreds of years later as a way of distinguishing one era from another. Encyclopedia wasn't fooled, and when he told why, Gus admitted he had made the pots himself, copying pictures he had seen in an old book.

Solution to *The Case of Grandma's Cookies*

When Ziggy and Encyclopedia approached Rocky, they only asked him if he had seen Ziggy's cookies. No mention was made of the kind of cookies they were. When Rocky said that he hoped they found the boy before he ate all the chocolate chip cookies, Encyclopedia knew he had been lying. Only if Rocky had opened the tin could he have known what kind of cookies they were.

Once Encyclopedia pointed this out, Rocky confessed he was the thief. He gave the cookies back to Ziggy.

A grateful Ziggy shared the cookies with Encyclopedia.

Solution to *The Case of the Grabbed Groceries*

Rusty said he had bought the groceries hours earlier. Yet he was nervous at the thought of Encyclopedia opening a can of soda near his face. The only reason for that would be because he expected the soda to shoot out if it was opened. That would only have happened if the cans had been shaken up recently—as they would have been if Rusty had been running with them back to the clubhouse only a few minutes before.

Faced with the prospect of being sprayed with a soda from the shaken cans, Rusty confessed to taking the groceries. He returned them to Ginger.

Solution to *The Case of the Giant Shark Tooth*

Unlike most animals with teeth, sharks don't keep their adult teeth for their whole life. They actually lose all their teeth every month or so when new ones grow in to replace the worn-out old ones. Therefore sharks' teeth do not get the chance to grow over time as Duke said.

When Encyclopedia confronted Duke with the facts, Duke admitted that he made the sharks' teeth himself. He had carved them out of wood and painted them white. His fake shark teeth ended up in the trash along with his dream of some quick cash.

Solution to *The Case of the Missing Medallions*

Mr. Cuthbert claimed that the glass had been broken by the thief standing outside the shop. But if the glass had been broken that way, the broken pieces would have fallen inside the shop onto the display case. However all the pieces of glass were outside the shop on the sidewalk. That meant the window had been broken from the inside—and only Mr. Cuthbert himself could have done that.

Encyclopedia caught the telltale clue of the glass. Mr. Cuthbert had to confess to having faked the crime. He hadn't planned it in advance, but when Winslow showed interest in the medallions, he thought he could throw suspicion onto him. Cuthbert had hoped to collect an insurance payment and then secretly sell the medallions as well. He needed the money because business had been bad.

Solution to *The Case of the Shipwreck*

It's a really hot summer day in Idaville, which lies in the Northern Hemisphere. According to Wilford, it was also a really hot day at the beach where his uncle was at the southern tip of South America, which is in the Southern Hemisphere. However, when it is summer in the Northern Hemisphere, it is winter in the Southern Hemisphere. The seasons are reversed. Thus anyone at the bottom of South America only a week earlier would be freezing in the middle of winter—not going to the beach.

When Encyclopedia pointed this out, Wilford admitted that he had made the story up. The only uncle he had lived in Nebraska.

Solution to *The Case of Mrs. Washington's Diary*

As Encyclopedia knew, it would have been quite a feat for George Washington's mother to write that someday her baby boy would be president. After all, he was born in 1732. At the time, there was no president, and no United States, either. Both of these things only came to be fifty-seven years later, after the Constitution of the United States had been adopted. Washington did become the first president in 1789, and his mother lived long enough to see him inaugurated.

When Encyclopedia informed him of his error, Jack admitted he had made the diary pages himself. He apologized to Sally and offered her anything she wanted in his booth for free. Sally found a nutcracker shaped like Teddy Roosevelt's head and took that instead. Her mother was delighted.